bracken

bracken

an anthology from the first five issues

Readers may contact the publisher at
brackenmagazine.com

This edition was prepared for publishing by
Ghost River Images
5350 East Fourth Street
Tucson, Arizona 85711
www.ghostriverimages.com

Cover art by Jana Heidersdorf
janaheidersdorf.com/

ISBN 978-0-578-48346-7

Library of Congress Control Number: 2019905323

Printed in the United States of America

June 2019

Bracken

an anthology from the first five issues

Anthology Editor	Charlotte d'Huart
Editor	Alina Rios
Poetry Editor	Jed Myers
Assistant Poetry Editor	Erin Slomski-Pritz
Assistant Fiction Editor	Charlotte d'Huart
Poetry Readers	Andrew Gordon Ted McMahon
Fiction Readers	Kimberly Huebner V. Wesley
Art Editor	Alina Rios
Graphic Designer	Kimberly Huebner
Social Media	Bridget Nee
Founders	Alina Rios Piper Robert

Introduction

What is your connection to the woods?

For me, it's mud-caked wellington boots after long walks through the English countryside, the earth damp and wormy and stamped with leaves, littered with plump chestnuts. It's hushed journeys into Floridian woods, heart racing at the thought of alligator eyes watching from still, green water, everything painted with the dusty finish of sunlight filtered through Spanish moss. It's the thick mist and springy moss of the Pacific Northwest, and towering cedars and firs stained black with lightning, and the whisper of crow wings above. And, of course, it's the Brothers Grimm and Fantastic Mr. Fox, Mirkwood and Brocéliande...

There's a reason storytelling has long found inspiration in the woods, whether as symbol or as setting. The forest can be a place of profound beauty or terror, a place of sustenance or danger, a place to find solitude or to become hopelessly lost, a place of magic and dark corners where the imagination can run wild.

It's the stories that arise from this convergence of the deeply personal and the universal that Bracken seeks to harvest. From the beginning, we've collected pieces that not only capture the magic and beauty of nature, but also explore encounters with those hidden spaces inside and outside us, those unknowable things that wink at us and shapeshift in the dark—encounters with both pain and wonderment and the journey between.

In putting this anthology together, we've wanted to take you on such a journey. We've selected and arranged work from past issues in a way that we think truly embodies Bracken's spirit. Just as the girl on our cover is emerging from the tangle of branches into the light, we want to let these pieces guide you from the forest's edge, through its depths, and out the other side. We hope you'll find something along the way.

Charlotte d'Huart
Anthology Editor

Contents

Resonances

by Cicely Gill

Before, I lived in woods, smelled leaves in bud
and knew a thousand words for green,
loved to sit cushioned by bright emerald moss
where slanting suns patterned my body
with shadows of twigs and branches,
an elemental camouflage, calming
as the trees' continuous pulse.
I could feel sap rise.

Before, I'd wait all day, present
to the imperceptible footfall of deer,
the ripple of blackbirds' wings.
I'd hear a moth alight.

Darkness my blanket, even without the moon
my fingers read each object, which plant, tree I touched,
this rough and warm, that coldly velvet
and from a branch aloft breathing the dawn
my skin sensed danger:
the silence of something rather than nothing.
Before, perhaps all that.
Now I know only that I love the woods.

Come with Me

by Ellie Davies

Zugunruhe

ornithological term for "migratory restlessness"

by Olivia V. Ambrogio

They shift and mutter in the dark
of their cages, the bars
an insubstantial lattice before the wheeling dome
of stars brightening ever earlier;
the magnet
drawing them like iron filings—a tug
through the breastbone
where the wing muscles tense—
pointing them, indifferent to perch
or seed or bath,
facing the way of travel

Yesterday the starlings poured across the sunset sky
in a shimmering river
endless currents made of flight
it flows through me still

At night
tossing and twisting in the sheets
I stare unseeing,
my mouth moves, searching
for other languages,
in my chest   a fluttering
that will not give me ease

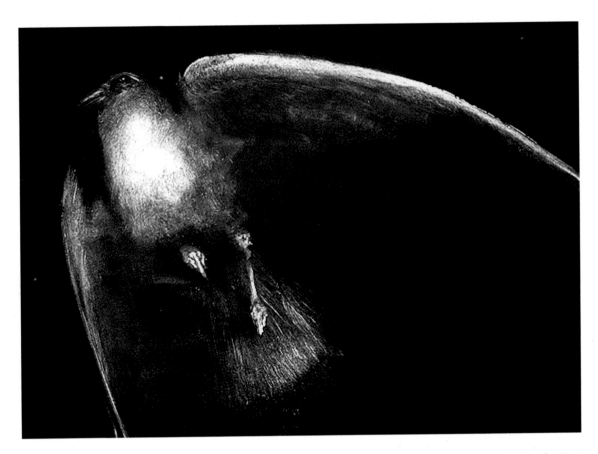

Flying Bird #4
by Bathsheba Veghte

Wild Ones

by Vanessa Fogg

Last week I saw *her* in the woods. I'd spent the day in copyedits for a client, and went for a walk to clear my head. I took the path behind my house, into the stands of beech and maple. The autumn wind stirred, so that golden leaves rustled above and all around me. Gold fell through the air and lined the path at my feet. And then *she* was suddenly there, blocking my way. She smiled, showing white pointed teeth. She wore a dress of rustling flame, and red leaves and berries were threaded through her golden hair. Her eyes were the fading green of summer's last days.

My heart went still; I couldn't breathe. And then my heart restarted, thudding hard.

"No," I told the Queen of the Hunt. It was a bare whisper, not the brave mother's defiance that I wanted. She laughed.

*

Each fall the Hunt returns. They take our children, the ones aged twelve to sixteen. They give our children the winds to ride, and lead them storming across the midnight sky.

No one in town speaks much of it. We say nothing when our kids start going to bed early, all on their own. We rouse them, still dazed, from sleep, and they drag themselves through the day. Teachers do not scold as students yawn and rub their eyes, as they slump and fall asleep at their desks.

We parents are tired, too, from nights pacing or standing outside bedroom doors, waiting for our kids to come back.

Amy sits blinking at breakfast. I've made scrambled eggs, gooey with melted cheese, and browned sausages and toast. She picks at it. It's still dark outside, and the kitchen light casts harsh shadows across her face. I want to fill her up with food, to weigh her thin body down. To tether her to this earth. Not to let her fly away.

Rick downs black coffee and kisses me quickly on the lips.

He doesn't usually hug Amy good-bye. Somewhere along the way we've all dropped the easy hugs and cuddles of childhood. He doesn't hug her now. But he reaches out and ruffles her hair. Her eyes focus, and she gives him a faint smile.

He leaves and it's just the two of us, she and I.

How was it last night? I want to ask. *Did you chase a flock of geese? How close did you come to the stars? Did you think of your father and me at all? Was it cold?*

I don't ask. My own mother never asked me.

"Take the heavier jacket," is all I say. She nods and shrugs on her thick padded coat. She walks out to the bus stop, through the dark.

*

It was always cold; I remember that. But I also remember that it didn't matter. It didn't matter because the Wild Ones called and the winds came. I spun like a leaf across the sky. My classmates were with me, all of us shrieking and diving and laughing. The cold poured into me and through me. My bones dissolved into darkness and air. The Wild Ones sang, and their song became part of me too: heartbeat and breath. The Great Hounds strained at their leashes and yelped, huge eyes glowing like campfires. *She* gave the signal. The Hounds raced forward, howling, and we came behind.

Everything fled before us; the tree-tops bent under our passage, and animals on the ground rushed from their hiding places: deer and rabbits and foxes, stray dogs and cats. Geese honked, owls panicked, ducks stirred on the water, while the songbirds went silent. We chased migrating flocks across the sky.

On and on and on. Wind and wildness and pure delight. I don't remember leaving the Hunt; I don't recall falling back to sleep in my own bed. But I must have. Each morning I woke back in my own room, under warm covers. My mother's hand on my shoulder, her voice saying my name.

*

I came back each time. But not everyone does.

Every so often, a child rides with the Hunt and never comes back.

*

After Amy leaves, I spend the morning cleaning. I vacuum the living room, dragging the couch forward to get at the layers of dust beneath. I wipe down the shelves and mantel. I mop the floor and light a vanilla-scented candle. I make everything warm and cozy, clean and safe.

The wind sings outside. Golden leaves whirl past the window. I watch the beech trees trembling, and wonder if I see a richer gleam of yellow among them. Or the flicker of a dress that rustles with red and orange flame.

"No," I tell her again. Queen of the Wild Ones, Queen of the Hunt. I won't let her take my child. I won't.

*

Rick holds me during these chilly nights. "She'll be fine," he murmurs into my hair. "Amy's got a good, level head—just like her parents."

But I think, *That's not enough.*

No one can predict it. There are years when no one is taken, and then years when multiple children are lost. Loners and troubled kids, quiet ones, forgotten ones. But also the popular kids, the golden ones, the cheerleader and sports star, the honor student and student council president. The kids who seem at home in the world, with loving family and friends.

It's always a choice, it's said. The Wild Ones take no one against their will. The Queen chooses a special few, for reasons that only she understands. She extends her invitation. Some accept.

Don't you remember? I want to ask my husband. *What it felt like to race the Hounds across the sky? To be part of that autumn storm?*

But if I ask, he'll claim not to remember. Just as so many adults claim. He never speaks of his days in the Hunt.

The wind whistles outside our bedroom window, and my skin prickles. I don't tell Rick that I'm not as level as he thinks. I don't mention the dreams I used to have, long after they should have stopped. Or that I met the Queen in the woods this season.

His breathing deepens and slows. I lie next to him, listening. Amy is out there, flying in the night. I think I hear voices, singing.

*

I throw myself into homemaking.

I turn down editing work a client offers. Instead, I chop vegetables and bake bread. I braise meat for stews. I try to make our home a beacon of warmth and light. An anchor for Amy. Something to call her back each night.

Beef bourguignon, lasagna, a pan of brownies. Lentil soup, spaghetti, and chicken pot pie. Her favorite dishes. The Wild Ones eat nothing but starlight and air, dead leaves and frost. They hunt only for the thrill. How could their food compare to that prepared with a mother's love?

Amy comes home from school, and I lure her to the kitchen table with mugs of hot chocolate, cookies, a bacon sandwich. We sit together in the autumn sun.

Once she told me everything. Once she was a toddler who babbled incessantly, a stream-of-consciousness narration, so that I sometimes yearned to pull a pillow over my head. And then she was a child, an eager schoolgirl who came to my study each day after school to spill all her thoughts. I knew the names of her friends and who was fighting with whom. I knew the jokes she'd heard that day. I knew which passage in a book had captured her heart.

I don't know these things now.

I ask about her day and she answers, but so much goes unsaid. Her eyes drift past me, fixed on another world.

It's normal, everyone says. Our children become quiet and absent in mid-autumn. But they come back.

Most of them come back.

I want to talk to her. Really talk. But the spell of these days is upon us both, and my throat closes when I try. I want to warn her of the Queen's offer. I want to tell her, *Don't say yes.* I want to say, *Stay with me.* But my thoughts slip and my mind fogs. The words dry on my lips.

I ask about her English homework instead. She answers, and even looks me in the eye. She finishes her sandwich. The light is shining on her light brown hair. Then she remembers something the English teacher said, a terrible pun of the type that she knows will make me groan, so she tells me and she's laughing and I groan and laugh, too. She's back, and I think it has to be enough—sunlight, laughter, shared food at the table. It has to be enough to keep her here.

*

This world is enough.

That's what I think when I'm alone in the house and I hear the Queen's voice from the woods. It's what I told myself for years of early adulthood, after the dreams finally stopped—when I'd left this town and went backpacking through Europe; when I studied in London; when I stood on a beach in Mexico under the moonlight, alone, watching the waves as my friends back at the hotel bar got drunk and flirted with strangers. It's what I felt when I met Rick. And it's what I tell myself now, when the wind rises and the old restlessness stirs. This world is enough. I don't need anymore. Amy doesn't need anymore. She has to know that.

*

I run to the woods to find *her*.

I take the path behind my house, down the hill. The trees close around me.

I reach the spot where I last saw her. Beams of sunlight slant through golden leaves.

I catch my breath, and all the trees rustle softly.

What do I have to offer? What can I give the Wild Queen? I have no jewels, no ring or necklace, to surpass her gold. I know no secret names. What bargain can I strike for my daughter's safe passage? What do I have?

Please, I think silently at her. *Please.*

Amy's come home safely three seasons in a row. But that's no guarantee. It's only more dangerous as our children get older. The pull grows stronger. She's fifteen now. More children are taken at this age than any other.

And the Queen has been watching our house. I've felt her. I saw her in these woods, for the first time in decades. It means something. She wants something.

"Not Amy," I say aloud.

She doesn't show herself, but the wind stirs in response. The wind strengthens. Branches lift, and trees fill with the sound of the sea; they are bending and roaring and golden leaves fly. Autumn is speaking. *She* is speaking. The sound fills my blood. But I can't understand it. I can no longer leap to the sky to follow her song.

*

Why do we forget so much of our wild days? How do we lose the language of the wind?

Why can't we talk of it, even to others who have survived?

I remember how it felt to skim my fingers along the bellies of clouds. To taste starlight and frost. To feel my heart turn ice-cold.

I remember the Queen as she rode. Her hair streaming white and silver in the moonlight, but streaked with flame. Her laughter, cold and ringing.

"She has a level head," Rick says of our daughter, and I pray that he's right. That she's more his daughter than mine. For if the Queen had given me the choice, I would have said Yes; I would have followed her back to her home in an instant.

*

I count the days down. Alone in my house, I draw the curtains closed and don't go to the woods again.

For two weeks in mid-autumn, the Hunt rides. Fourteen days, during which the moon waxes from its thinnest sliver to its full light. Each night the sound of the Hounds baying. The songs and cries of the Wild Ones.

During these last days, I do what I can to pull my family close. I make popcorn after dinner. I coax Rick and Amy to the living room with a movie. I pull out an old board game Amy loves. I try to keep us up late, together against the night.

"Let her go," Rick whispers to me when Amy rolls her eyes, when she yawns and says that she's tired and going to bed.

I cling to him to quell the shaking inside.

The wind is so strong now. I'm long past my wild years. I settled down before Amy was born. I'm a middle-aged woman in the suburbs, a wife and mother. Old and earth-bound. But when the wind calls, I feel like it might blow me away, too.

*

On the last night of the Hunt, against all custom, I go outside to watch.

High above, I see it ride. Flashes of light through the clouds. Moonlight mixed with darkness.

And I know that Rick is right—there is nothing I can do. If she's picked, Amy will make her own choice.

The clouds part, and the Hunt swoops down. I see the milk-white Hounds, their red eyes burning. The Wild Ones shining, moonlight in their faces and their hair trailing sparks of flame. Their calls so high and piercing. And between Hounds and Wild Ones, flitting and diving in shadows, are the children.

They all sweep toward me, and the noise is deafening. I feel the wind on my face. I see the Queen, her face cold and inhumanly beautiful. I almost make out the moonlit faces of the children. I see their nightgowns fluttering, their flannel pajamas and t-shirts.

The Hunt swirls above my head, then stills.

The Queen lifts her hand, and one by one, the children leave. I see their shadow-figures slipping away toward the dark houses below them. They're going home. Is Amy among them? Amy—

The Queen turns and looks directly at me. She extends her hand.

At last, I understand.

I stare into her shining eyes and know that it's not too late, after all. I'm not too old. I have this second chance.

I hear Amy's voice: "Mom!" But if I reach for the Queen's hand, I'll fly again. I'll ride the winds. I'll be forever wild.

The Girl with the Flower Crown

by Amanda Greive

Prayer (1)

by Lucy Harlow

sky of all elsewheres
—fever-bright late light on your ragged
hems of searing day, your clouds scorched-tree-scored
with branches' shadows, your heft and weft
marvelously woven, though star-weighted, ship-snagged
and tired with use—

do you grow weary of my habitual petitions
insisting, as they do, on your veil-like attributes,
imploring past you and through you and
implying that you are not
what you are,
but what you hide?

*

because I do. It is very wearisome
to be at all times imprecise
and in all ways insufficient,
the nothing in me fathoming drowned mercy
in the nothing in you,
a rendezvous of nothings meeting in
your infinite horizons' haze—

let me breathe, then:
breathe, only.

let me sound my underground lakes and airy chambers
and send my breath to your breath,
and know
chance words decay far, far below
your sapphire peaks and starless ravines
of deep space.

*

sit you down, oh Orpheus, sit you down
and lift your harpist's fingers to the loom
and weave:
twist on the lucet-lyre your voice
and breathe a song, upon
your warp-harp the nether sky.

listen only with your wet tongue:
taste the immutable unknowable, and the
immortal elsewhere.

Understory

by Sierra Golden

Lord, there are creatures under my skirt.
Butterflies, of course. Their fluttering, whorled wings
familiar and fickle and fragile. And bright-eyed rabbits,
fear striking them into a trembling stillness and flight.

The slugs I love and their trails of slime.
I study the way one nibbles another
and a pair will climb above the forest floor
to hang from a branch on a rope of mucus.

Before they drop back to the ground, there is this
unbound departure from life as they know it:
both male, both female, both unfold translucent glowing
sexes and weave them into the flaring petals of a rose.

I'm beginning to know the snakes too, smelling like earth
and flicking forked tongues on my thighs, but Lord
I must be a terrible keeper—other creatures cluster
under my skirt too and I don't even know their names.

Unwritten taxonomies live in my dark. Lord,
I need to know how shall I love them hidden and crooked?
They bite with daggered teeth or they have no teeth.
They look like dragons and feel like clouds or tentacles

or tusks. They swim. They fly. They sit still as a rock.
I wear gloves and boots and watch as they starve.

Run

by Henry Hu

Just When You Think You Know Everything

by Jenifer Browne Lawrence

One day I was listening to the AM radio, driving out the road in my dad's half-ton Chevy on my way to meet Norman. Carole King and I were singing *Smackwater Jack*. I shifted down to third coming into the curve where black glacier rock rises up on the left and the ground drops off to the water on the right. The mist rose up like it usually did, from rainwater sheeting down the rock face, making rainbows you could drive through. The spray covered my windshield and I fiddled around for the wiper knob. And doesn't everything happen just when you're not looking?

I'm meeting Norman at Outer Point. I have the poles, and he has the herring and beer. Of all the boys I've kissed, Norman is the only one who hasn't tried to unzip my pants. Though for him, I might. But he's only interested in catching the next fish. Norman has his own boat, a Grady White. It used to be his Dad's before he drowned two winters ago off of Kodiak. Norman's brother Gunnar was supposed to get the boat but quit fishing after the accident. Today though, we're casting from shore. We're going to build a fire and wait for the tide to come in. Probably hook a few Dollies, maybe a Coho if we're lucky. It's too foggy to see the water. Just about everything is gray here—gray or green, or black—sky, trees, rock. Bear? A black bear is standing in the road, up on its hind legs, looking at me. I'm braking hard, thinking oh, it's just a cub, though it was bigger, a yearling, maybe. Thinking Dad's going to kill me if I wreck the truck, thinking I'll be late and Norman will think I'm not coming. Somehow the Chevy slides past the bear, it's moving, too, and I come to a stop and watch out the side window as the bear heads into the brush—blueberry, salmonberry, devil's club. Skunk cabbage. If you're a bear, what's not to like?

A big ka-thump in the back of the truck bounces me in the seat. I look in the rearview. It's another bear. It's in the bed, in the fucking truck bed. Roy Orbison is singing, *pretty woman, kind I'd like to meet, don't walk away, hey.* The bear's backside fills the window. I lock the door. I can smell the bear. It reminds me of Lonnie's shepherd, Jeb, washed up on the bank at Lemon Creek. Lonnie's dog had gotten smacked by a porcupine. His dad pulled the quills but the dog went back after it every time he got loose, and limped home full of needles, and Lonnie's dad said he'd had just about enough of that shepherd. When they got Jeb out of the water the quills spiked out from his muzzle like one of those old masks at the museum. I can smell my sweat, too, mixed with the bear stink. The bear's turning around. It fits in the truck bed no problem, just another yearling.

There's a back-to-school sale at Behrend's, the radio announcer says. He says there's seventeen days until school, says enjoy the sunshine, it's going to be hot, maybe 75, says the sun's going down at 10:03, two minutes earlier than yesterday. The sun hasn't broken through yet. I have Dad's old Army blanket for the beach, and a pair of cutoffs just in case. The smart bear is still in the brush, stripping blueberries. In the back of the truck the other bear's breath is fogging the glass. Its teeth are really clean, yes and big, but so white. I can't stop looking. It lifts onto its back legs and I'm staring at its belly, maybe it's a girl, then it's over the cab and climbing down, swinging its backside at me as it lumbers into the woods. My dad's going to freak about the scratch marks on the hood. Gouges, I should say. No way I'm getting out to check the roof. I twist around in my seat. There's an eye knocked loose on one of the salmon rods, but it's not at the tip, we can still fish with it. I let the clutch out too fast. The truck lurches but doesn't die—it's foolproof, my dad says, and don't pass anyone, he says, and be home by dark, and that's not so hard in summertime and by next winter I'll be seventeen and can stay out as late as I want, like my sister.

I pull over behind Norman's VW minibus. He sleeps in it sometimes, when his mom and brother are fighting. He's built the fire already. He's sitting on a driftwood log, squinting at the smoke. "A bear jumped into the truck," I say, handing him the good pole. "Yeah, right." Norman says, and pulls me onto the log. "What happened to your pole?" I stand up again, even though I'm feeling kind of wobbly. "It did. I think it jumped off the waterfall rock. It climbed right over me. Did you know bears have really clean teeth?" Norman shakes his head, reaches for my hand. My teeth are chattering. "Bears don't jump." I pull him up from the log, drag him toward the truck. "Holy shit," he says. "Fuck. Are you okay?" We're looking at the claw marks on the hood. My whole body's shivering, and then I start crying. Norman dries my cheeks with his coat sleeve. We sit by the fire and drink some beer, watching a wavy line of pollen drifting toward us on the tide.

Visitation

by Rebecca Hart Olander

In the folds of old flannel
draped over my closet door,
my father's face manifest, wizened
in profile, knob-nosed and knowing,
a Germanic folk tale illustration.

When I look close, he's disappeared
back into the underbrush,
unblinking eyes watching me
from so deep in bracken, I can only catch
the slightest scent on the sleeves.

I grasp for more,
but it is crumbs left in the wood,
glinting in moonlight,
illuminating the way,
no matter how hard I try to get lost.

Sleeper

by Constantinos Chaidalis

That Willow

by Kathryn Hunt

Above that willow only stars and we
lay under, two whispered girls, half-blind

in the half-light, the long occult
branches, cool seep of earth against

our backs. Hatchlings, our breasts
not even breasts yet, bee stings,

tender as the mouth we saw
Marilyn Monroe make in the movies.

Mandy Goodpasture,
Mandy Goodpasture, girl I chased into

a swayback barn to kiss on heaps of
fresh-shorn hay and loll about in sifted

light, those ravening hours, the rafters
white with pigeon poo: O girl

who kissed me back, where are you now?
Under the willow we looked up

to see the stars fall one by one,
counted them, kept score, wanting

to defeat each other. I imagined in that
great expanse my life unwinding into space

until I disappeared and only stone and
fire and something else—voiceless,

mountain cold, full of real mercy—
touched me. I could not account for it,

the way it held and cast me out,
as if it breathed me. That tree: I saw

it had been cut down when I drove by,
its groan, gone under a neighbor's saw,

the stars carried in its crown falling
a second time, and in the yellow grasses

the place where we lay dreaming, the years
we traveled distantly already in us.

Moth

by Constantinos Chaidalis

Her Hands Like Ice

by KT Bryski

The hands of the vampire-hunter move like spiders, and I hate them. They creep over our kitchen table, avoiding the plates of sausage and country bread my mother has laid out. They scuttle along the sides of a polished walnut case. Quick fingers, sly fingers—they lift belts and let brass buckles fall with a clink, clink, clink. They ease the lid up. Inside, his tools rest on velvet the colour of old blood. My mother chokes on a gasp; my father will not look.

I hate how the hands of the vampire-hunter dart this way and that as he lays out his instruments, caressing each like a lover.

Holy water.

Bullets.

Pistol.

Garlic.

Knife.

And smoothly, without a moment's pause: the stake.

At the sight of this last, my mother clutches my father's arm, her round face terrified in the candlelight.

"It won't hurt," the vampire-hunter says quietly.

My mother whimpers.

"Remember, it is not your daughter." He glances to me. "Not your sister, Marit."

I can only stare at his hands. They do not look like butcher's hands.

"She has not bitten?" he asks.

My parents do not answer, so I say, "No."

"Then I will watch for her tonight." The vampire-hunter's hands replace his tools into the polished walnut case. At the door, he pauses.

"Tomorrow, I will end it."

"Elisabeth," I say.

"I'm sorry?"

"Her name is Elisabeth."

He meets my hard stare, his grey eyes cool and calm. "Tomorrow." One final pause, his neat fingernails rapping the doorframe. "Mind, your hearth is dying."

*

Elisabeth returned three days after she died, her winding sheet flapping behind her like a bridal train. Falling snow half-covered her; she appeared and re-appeared, shining like ice and then disappearing into darkness.

"Elisabeth," I called in a cracked whisper.

She did not move, did not speak. My older sister shone brilliant in the moonlight, brighter than the unbroken snow, and then she passed into shadow. Beyond my reach, once again.

*

As I lie in bed, that first sighting washes over me. There is too much space without my sister. If I close my eyes, I see her again. I feel the snow biting my skin.

But most of all, I see her: gone before me in all things, even this last. I see her hands like ice, her arms thin and brittle as the trees' bare branches.

At such thoughts, I cannot sleep. In the moon's pale light, I dress myself. My hands dance over buttons and hooks as shrewdly as those of the vampire-hunter. Downstairs, the hearth sits grey and dead.

I do not re-stoke it. I take my cloak and leave the house without a sound.

The vampire-hunter waits at the end of the lane. He waits like a wolf, his head raised and eyes unblinking. The stake pokes up from his belt; his clever hands hold his pistol.

"Marit." He does not look at me. "What are you doing here?"

"I want to help."

A flicker of attention, nothing more. "You have seen her before, haven't you?'

I nod.

"Who else?" His voice is soft as the snow pluming around my boots. "Who else has seen her?"

"Our neighbours." I have spotted his walnut case resting at his feet, and now I cannot look away. "Customers at my father's brewery. I don't know how many."

"Who saw her first?"

"My father." My breath hangs in the air between us, alongside the lie.

The hands of the vampire-hunter fall to his stake. "If you saw her first, what would you do?"

"What?"

"Your father hoped he was dreaming. He said nothing. He waited until others had seen. Only then did he tell your mother. Only then did they send for me."

The winter presses close.

"What would you have done?" the vampire-hunter asks.

Before I can answer, he turns. Through snow and moonlight, Elisabeth appears. Her pointed face lifts as though scenting the air.

I am very cold.

Unlike me, Elisabeth does not trudge through the snow. She passes over it, leaving no trace. As she draws near, I strain forward. The vampire-hunter's arm shoots out, catching me in the chest.

"Be silent," he murmurs. "Be still."

It is a foolish thing to say. All my words freeze and catch between my teeth. And so I am silent, I am still, and my older sister glides past us. We are far from the village proper, and before Elisabeth is halfway there, she slips into the moonlight like so much scattered snow.

As the vampire-hunter lowers his arm, I exhale.

His long fingers play with the stake once again. "How many has she bitten?"

"None."

The vampire-hunter's gaze flicks to my throat, to where my fingers run in nervous circles over my own cold skin. "Go home, Marit," he says softly. "There is nothing you can do tonight."

His words stop me. "But tomorrow?"

"I will open her coffin at noon."

*

Elisabeth died after the soil had frozen. Tearful and desperate, my parents built fires over the planned gravesite, but the earth did not thaw. They laid her in the charnel house instead: a squat stone building in the corner of the churchyard. In summer, it stands empty. In winter, it holds the dead the ground will not receive.

That day, I sat at the kitchen table, alone. In clenched hands, I held her neckerchief. Though the warmth had left it, it smelled like her still. Cinnamon and woodsmoke. Smells I did not want to forget, even as the hearth-fire stuttered and smouldered and died to nothingness.

*

As I near the churchyard, my chest aches. It has ached for so long, it has simply become part of me, as the cold is part of winter.

The vampire-hunter waits outside the door to the charnel house. In his hands, he holds his walnut case. I do not look at it. Instead, I tug the door's iron ring. Wood scrapes over snow as the door opens, and a rush of cold hits me.

I step onto the stone floor. The vampire-hunter follows me silently. There is space enough that he need not stand too close. Recesses in the walls hold plain wooden coffins. I do not like the air in here—though it is scented only with snow's sharpness—so I take small breaths.

There are no windows, no openings. It is a cell, a vault, a meat cellar. I stare at my sister's coffin, my fingers curling at my sides. The hands of the vampire-hunter flash at the corner of my eye. He strikes a match along the stones.

It will not catch. He tries another, and another, but this dead place admits no light, no warmth. He tosses his last match aside with a frown.

"My breakfast was cold this morning," he says.

I prop the door open. Weak sunlight slants into the charnel house. Not enough to banish the shadows. Enough that the buckles of the walnut case gleam.

The vampire-hunter shakes himself. "Which is your sister's coffin?"

I point.

The hands of the vampire-hunter stroke her coffin. They rub the hinges. I want to scream.

I hate the hands of the vampire-hunter. I hate them as they lift the coffin lid. I hate them more when they fall limp and useless. I hate them most when they beckon me closer.

"Be silent," the vampire-hunter whispers hoarsely. "Be still."

For so my sister lies: unspeaking, unmoving. Her dark hair flows over her shoulders like oil on snow. But it is not my sister's hair. It does not have the sheen, the warmth. It is the hair of someone I do not know.

I lean over the open coffin. It is Elisabeth's face, but it is not Elisabeth's face, and I have never been so cold. The vampire-hunter's long fingers hook under her lips, pull them upwards, pull them back.

Small teeth, crooked teeth. The left incisor chipped from the time she tripped into my father's brew kettle. Harmless teeth. Human teeth.

"Not a vampire," the vampire-hunter breathes.

I yearn to put her lips back into place. "What, then?"

One by one, he inspects her fingernails. He brushes her hair aside, examines her neck. Then he wipes his hands on his trousers, frowning.

"What is she?" I ask again.

"I am not sure." Kneeling, he opens his case. "But we will be cautious, you and I."

There is no blood, because my sister is long dead. I do not look away. I do not cover my ears against the crack of the pistol and crunch of bone. When it is over, holy water stains my sister's winding sheet. A hole tears through her heart to match my own. Garlic spills from her slack mouth. The vampire-hunter passes a hand between her head and her neck, making sure.

"It is over," the vampire-hunter tells me, but his hands move ceaselessly, and I do not believe him.

*

"It is over," my mother told me, that last afternoon. I did not believe her, even as the fevered flush faded to grey. I did not believe her, for Elisabeth was still in my arms.

"Come back," I whispered. As though my breath would stir her to life again. As though she were only in need of stoking. "Please, come back."

Already, my sister's skin was so very, very cold.

*

Because I cannot think what else to do, I return home. My father leans over his brew kettle. "He took care of her, then?" he asks, not meeting my gaze.

I start to nod, but then I stop. I cannot smell the cloying sick-sweetness of boiling wort. No steam curls from the kettle's mouth. Edging beside my father, I lay one hand on its copper side.

Cold metal bites my skin.

"Why didn't you light the fire?" I ask.

My father blinks. When he speaks, his breath hangs before me. "What do you mean, Marit?"

"The wort, it's—" I push past him to the mash tun. Inside its wooden skirt, the copper tub sits lifeless. Wet grain slides through my fingers, slimy and chill.

My father leans over the brew kettle, inhaling. "It'll be a good batch," he says. Ice glints from the depths of his beard.

I run. Down the lane, towards the village proper. Chimneys stab the bright sky like fingers. No curls of smoke lie against the blue. At the blacksmith's, I stop. Clanging metal shatters the muffled quiet. If he is working, the forge must be lit. It must be.

I creep inside his shop. Sunlight shines off whitewashed walls. The blacksmith stands over his anvil, striking again and again. As the floorboards creak beneath my feet, he glances up. Frost coats his cheeks so that they gleam.

"Marit!" he says. "Is your sister...at rest?"

The metal rod on his anvil is dark, stiff. He beats it uselessly. The forge sits empty and shadowed. Setting his hammer to one side, the blacksmith pumps the great bellows behind the forge. A blast of cold air blows my hair back. Sticking the rod into the dead forge, he smiles.

"Go home, Marit, where it's warm."

*

I do not remember the days between Elisabeth's funeral and her return. I do not think I slept. I know I did not eat. I stayed in our bedroom, sitting on the cold floorboards. The chill leached through my stockings and petticoats.

"Come back. Please. Please come back."

*

"What is she?" I burst into the vampire-hunter's room at the inn. A leather trunk sits open on his bed. The hands of the vampire-hunter move things into it. Cravats and woollen socks, books and paper. His walnut case waits by the door.

"What do you mean?" His eyes are tired, and they do not meet mine.

"My sister is not a vampire. But—" I gesture to his empty hearth, the coals heaped useless as blocks of ice. "What is she doing?"

"It isn't her."

I blink.

"Marit." The hands of the vampire-hunter reach for me, and I recoil. "She is dead."

"Then what—"

"They are terribly cold, those first few days." The vampire-hunter looks at me askance. "Aren't they? Those first few days after."

I stare at him. And then it rushes over me, as merciless as the winter snows. The cold, empty nights: the fading scents of cinnamon and wood-smoke. I am sitting on the hard floorboards, and I am standing in the charnel house. I am letting her cold fingers fall from mine.

The hands of the vampire-hunter trip over themselves. They pick up his walnut case. They fumble with his coat. And then they falter on the doorknob.

"When you get home," he croaks, "build a fire. The biggest fire you can. Good luck."

"You're leaving?"

"I cannot help." The hands of the vampire-hunter ward me off, and I hate them more than ever. "She is no vampire. She is dead...or would be, if you only let her go."

For a long time, I stand motionless. Then, slowly, I walk home. Clouds have rolled in. It is that suspended time between afternoon and twilight—that peculiar greyness that happens only in winter. Snow drifts down, shrouding the earth in a winding sheet of its own.

Our house is no warmer. A pot hangs over the empty hearth. My mother sits in the parlour, her chair pulled close to the frozen woodstove. Ice seals her closed eyes.

I find matches in the kitchen. I strike them on the hearth stones, over and over, but they do not light. They snap between my fingers, rigid and brittle as dried bones. My eyes remain dry, terribly so, as I gather myself and try again.

I try to remember my sister's warmth. I remember the kicks to my ankle, my name on her lips. Above all, I remember cinnamon and woodsmoke.

The matches do not light. When I am down to the last one, the door creaks open.

Elisabeth glides in, her face too white in the fading light. Her winding sheet trails ice along the floor, and despite myself, I inch backwards. At my retreat, her pale lips lift. Her teeth are still the ones I knew so well. Small, crooked.

Harmless. Human.

"Elisabeth," I begin, but nothing else comes.

My sister's hands move like spiders, and I have missed them. They creep along our pitted kitchen table, avoiding the plates of stone-cold sausage, the country bread like an ice block. They wrap around mine, like ice. But I smell cinnamon and woodsmoke, and I sigh. A warm breath, as though she were only in need of stoking.

Come back, Elisabeth's eyes say. Please, come back.

My sister's hands stroke my cheeks. Quick fingers, gentle fingers—they place the match between my own. We drag it across the hearthstones.

Flame flares in the darkness. I hold the match close to me. A tiny pinprick of light, nothing more than that. Then I toss it in the hearth. The flame catches on grasses, catches on bark and kindling, and then the bigger logs are alight.

The warmth takes hold, and as my sister fades, her hands grasp mine.

My sister's hands, melting into mine like snow under the sun.

Darkness

by Jana Heidersdorf

Janitor of the Labyrinth

by Anita K. Boyle

My quarters are centered in the middle
of the maze. Each evening, an hour
past dusk, my broom-cart echoes
into the corridor. If I keep one eye
on the right wall, the labyrinth
becomes a kind of sphere, always
turning in on itself, so
I can return to where I began.

My broom sweeps every corner
throughout the long nights. Often,
the kindly stars light my way.
But even during the blindness
of moonless, cloud-filled nights,
experience shows the way.

A lost soul or two will
wander up in the darkness.
They are always a bit terrified,
confused, often weeping. I give them
silent signals to follow.
If they complain that the sweeping
and picking-up of refuse
dropped along the aisles
is too slow, I am tempted
to lose them. But if I do,
I generally have to scour
up their fusty parts
the next evening. Sometimes,

I run into them again. They
may be angry and shout hysterically,
fingers pointing. My response
is simple—wordless, I sweep
them to the side until they
are scrabbling along the walls
behind me, the dust causing them
to cough and sneeze. They are quieter
that way, and more complacent.

Near morning, I push the broom-cart
up a high ramp, and dump it
over the side. This is a job I love.
From the rim of the labyrinth,
the landscape is endless,
like an ocean.

If stragglers trail behind me until
morning, they will see the beauty
of the sun streaming over
the tall walls—mists and rainbows
refracting, dancing. This
makes them exceedingly happy,
though the Minotaur
will be lurking nearby.

By morning, the labyrinth clean,
I always arrive safely to my door.
I go inside, eat, then sleep,
and dream of the horizon line
visible after I've dropped my holy
collection of filth and ugliness.
I waken to the sound
of cloven hooves on cobbles.

Passing Through

by Stephen Thom

"It's nothing to do with that," she replied. Her voice was calm and measured, but her hand slid across the table towards him, forefinger tapping at the wood with increasing force. "It's that you keep finding a way to fuck everything up."

K stiffened in his chair, clenched his fork, and pushed a lump of potato on an aimless tour round his plate. There was a silence.

"Why," he muttered, "are you being such a complete and utter bitch tonight?"

The forefinger stopped tapping. She leaned forward. "I'm not talking about this. I'm not talking about this... this, us, I'm fed up to fuck of talking about it. I've accepted it. Everyone else has accepted it. It's only you that won't seem to fucking accept it. You fucked it up, just like you fuck everything up."

"Don't say that to me," K whispered.

"You're a liar."

"Don't fucking say that to me."

"You're a liar."

"Don't say that to me!"

Her hand had crept towards the edge of his plate. K didn't mean to—he didn't think he'd meant to—but he brought his fork down as he shouted, and saw the prongs puncture her skin. He saw a trail of little red beads; saw her screaming and thrashing around by the sink, grabbed his jacket from the kitchen door peg, and left.

*

He loped down the garden path and crunched onto the long stretch of road outside his home. It trailed off into the distance, surrounded on either side by flat, black panels of field; disappearing at the skirt of the night sky.

The cold stung his cheeks, and he thrust his hands into his pockets and tried to hit a pacy stride. Pacy enough to push through the feverish angst bubbling behind his forehead. Slick night silence washed around him. Breath left his mouth as a thin vapour, and sharp repetitions of phrases sparked round his mind. The organization and sense in her sentences collapsed, and he could only hear aggrieved sounds - peaks in pitch, resonating vowels hanging at the end of barked utterances. Her face was less and less fixed - increasingly a warped, irrelevant shroud, diluted through the dissonant sounds.

Through the clamouring, an angular shape gestated. It writhed at the fence to the left of the road. K paused. Crisp huffing and yelps sifted towards him, and with several more steps the struggling shape gained clarity. A man was tangled up in the fence.

K padded onto the grassy rise aside the road and gripped the cold fence to steady it. The man stopped and turned. Although the majority of his body was through the fence, his left leg was wedged between the two middle stretches of wire. Closer now, K could see his trousers were caught on two barbed twists.

"Got yourself in a bit of a fix," K muttered as he eased along the fence towards him.

"Yeah." The man stopped tugging, and slumped onto the grass. He rolled onto his back and wiggled his trapped leg. Looking down, K took in his thin face, reddened by the cold. His eyes were deep-set, larger than most, and notably far apart, giving space to a long nose that rose above a tiny, thin-lipped mouth. K had trouble focusing on his eyes. He felt, for the briefest of moments, that they might have been entirely white.

"It's my leg, my damned leg," the man sighed.

"I can see that. Here, you just need to -"

K slipped the folds of fabric from the tiny spikes, and the man jerked his leg free, sprang to his feet and exhaled. Rubbing his hands together, K glanced up and down the dark road. Several white lines in the centre offered the only colour around. They might have been the only two people in the world.

"What were you - what are you doing out here?" asked K, immediately struck by the feeling he might regret it.

"I think... just passing through," nodded the man. He flicked a spindly finger at the fence. "I keep doing that to myself." Then abruptly, he turned to K and proffered his hand.

"Thank you, thank you for that. You have a good night now."

It was said with such finality that K felt any further small talk sucked out of him. He took the man's hand and they engaged in a brief, solemn shake, whereafter the man turned away and looked up. K squinted at him for a moment, then slid his way down the wet grass back onto the road. He walked several paces, confused, and muddling the idea of throwing a 'good bye' or 'good luck' back. Yet, when he looked round, the man was staring at the sky with such intensity that he felt he would only be interrupting.

K strode on into the tunnel of shadows, and waited at a discreet distance before glancing back again. The grassy rises became black lumps, the fields around were endless oceans, and the crooked shape of the strange man, standing and staring, was silhouetted against the sick light of the stars and moon.

His memories of the argument—obliterated by the tangled trousers—swam back out of the murkiness, and temporarily he was lost again in broken words and gestures. The next time he thought to glance back, the man was gone. He was sure he could still make out the stretch of fence, but no skinny figure holding a vigil. No cars had been past. Perhaps he had moved on. Perhaps he had remembered which way he was going.

I keep doing that to myself.

When K returned home, she was gone. He found a couple of scrunched-up note attempts in the kitchen bin.

*

He returned to the house only once after moving out, some twenty years later. News of her passing had filtered through to him, and although he bypassed the funeral, he found himself giving way to an irresistible, melancholic pull that reeled him onto a train and back to their old country home.

The dying afternoon was still warm as he stepped up the garden path. Weeds snaked amongst the soil. His hand rested on the door handle, the wind played with wisps of his thinning hair, and he felt as if he should have remembered it differently. There were windows, set in the white walls to his left and right. Had there always been two windows above those? He had the warped sensation of viewing a hologram, or a much smaller house, or that he was in entirely the wrong place.

Inside, the hall felt damp and oppressive, and the patterns on the wallpaper had faded into abstract bursts. The kitchen was set out as he knew it; patches of light leaked over the table and far wall, and he shuffled between them. He leaned beside the sink and watched the wooden chair squared away at the centre of the table, where she had sat when he had last seen her. He studied the dusty curve of its back, the floral imprints. Everything in this house looked so small.

He squinted and tried to project her onto her chair. He had been projecting her everywhere since that last night, and he would continue doing so for what little time remained. Days, months, and years had collapsed beneath him and, as he squeezed his eyes tighter, hopelessly willing some kind of final picture, droplets wet the deep lines under them.

K rubbed a shaking arm against his nose, clung to the sink, and reached down to tug open the utensil drawer. He pulled out several knives and hurled them onto the floor. Night was seeping in and the wind had picked up outside, rattling the window, as he took his place at the table with a single fork. He spread his right hand out on the wooden surface. His left hand was shaking so much now that he had trouble positioning the fork above it. Steeling himself, he raised his arm and motioned to thrust the fork down. By the time it landed his will had failed him. The prongs tapped at his wrinkled skin, leaving the tiniest of indentations.

K looked at the chair across from him again. The shadows seemed to bleed into thick shapes within the confines of its dusty curves. He pulled himself up and stumbled quickly out of the house, holding onto the walls for support.

The wind propelled him along the narrow road, and the moon suffused the fields on either side of him with a muddied glow. He stuck close to the scrappy grass at the edge, bouncing threads of history, and reimagined history, and ruined, obliterated history behind his eyes. Whilst he stumbled on into the familiar shadow tunnel that grew away from the house, he saw two convoluted shapes shifting in the rises to the side of the road. Black shapes separated from finer layers of black, and hoarse voices mingled with the wind.

K felt drawn to and comforted by all this as he clambered up onto the grassy hump. The ground had the consistency of fudge, and he reached for the metal support of the fence. Groping along it, he navigated his way towards the wriggling shapes. It was men. Two men, lying on the ground. Their legs were trapped in the fence. A bluster of wind flung K against the wires, and he slumped to his knees beside them.

"You're stuck?" he shouted above the rumble. "Your legs, are you stuck?"

Closer now, he could make out the two rigid, grey faces as they turned towards him. The mouths were tiny and thin-lipped. But it was the eyes, clear white eggs, that shook him.

"Yes, our legs," the man closest to him said, rubbing his hands into boggy folds of soil. His voice was thin and had an odd, metallic quality to it. The second man laughed abruptly—a sharp, ringing sound.

K reached towards the fence and unclipped the segments of trouser fabric twisted onto barbed spikes. The wind caressed his shaking hands and he felt safe in the familiarity of the task, in the vicinity of his old home. For the briefest of moments he indulged in the snowball of memories, snippets of interactions, and mental photographs.

When they were freed, the two men jumped up and wiped off the dirt on their clothes. K rose to join them. The wind had calmed, and a hush fell over the road.

"I think I remember you," he said, "or at least one of you. I think this happened before."

"It's possible," replied the man to his left. His white eyes gleamed in the moonlight. "There are times when we are passing through." He turned to the fence and patted it. "We keep doing this to ourselves, though."

The second man laughed again; a grating sound.

K opened his mouth to reply, but both men were rooted to the spot, staring at the sky. The time for talking appeared to be over, and they took no more notice of him. As K traipsed away, a fine rain wet his scalp, and when he looked around, the men were gone. He was unsurprised by this, and in truth he had been expecting it. It was absurd. Yet he found himself missing them, and their clumsiness, and the way they had stopped him thinking about awful times.

The dot of the house was still visible in the distance through the slanting rain. He wondered how it was possible that he could have found it within himself, so easily, to say and do things that hurt someone he loved so much... it was absurd.

The house would be there when he closed his eyes again, as everything would be.

We are passing through.

We keep doing this to ourselves.

"all that is left of yesterday"

by Michael Marsh

Prayer, Apostrophe

by Bryce Emley

Tell me what you know about salt,
how speech can be a kind of thirst.

I could swear that once I heard my name
as rain caught the fingers of pine trees,
that I heard tide whisper into shoreline,
I am. I am.

Tell me, is it holy to speak,
so much fluid in the lungs?
That when I listen long enough
I hear a voice underwater, feel
the Dead Sea pooling in my throat?

Tale from the Vienna Woods
by Erika Michael

Skulking vulpine, amber tail —
           in the woods the vixens wail.
        Brown-rimmed halo crowns a ragged moon —
                              rugged forestland suffused
     in gloom.

Where does evil work begin?

        Fleetingly on briar-thorn the shimmer of a
rictus grin   catches hair
                              and scraps of skin —

           shattered mother, barren bride
ravaged by a crow
                    and thrown   aside.

I hear the rooster shrieking   *crock-a-too*
                 blood is pouring from the shoe
                 blood is pouring from the shoe

     Boney fingers spread their greeting
          from a coven
                              woo the wanderers with gingerbread —
                    throw children in the oven.

     Swaying school bells stalk my dream.
           I hear sirens but   evade
the searchlight beams.
                         Shadow men with pounding feet fly
        along a lamplit street —   road to nowhere
        though way is clear,
                    the end is fraught with fear.

Flint-eye squatters occupy the trees
fixed to storm,   to rise
to begin their thundering   flight
screaming   whining
raptors now discharge into the
skies over rooftop, playfield, schoolyard,
up into the piercing light

down into the bogged blight they
speed
to an abyss where foxes feed.

Helmet-headed troops unloosed
in the land — the ravens roost.

As I awake, a hoary specter snags
a child. I hear the din —
her will is strong,   the tale is grim.
The merry widow waltzes to
a requiem.
I know the steps but can't begin.   I'm
strangely on the

outside
looking in.

Bracken

by Jana Heidersdorf

I Am Your Rabbit

by Bo Balder

The new King clambers up the platform to greet his subjects. He's young and swarthy, already paunchy like his brother, the more famous Bonaparte. I, Gretl, and my brother Hans the Hatter have come to see his ascension to the throne. The King lifts his hands and speaks. A stifled laugh rises from the gathered crowd. It's not the fact that he speaks Dutch—that's exceedingly polite for a foreign king. It's the words he speaks.

"I am your rabbit," Louis-Napoleon says.

The Butcher next to us explains in a penetrating whisper that he meant to say "I am your king" in Dutch, but that his French accent made it sound like this ludicrous statement. My brother and I exchange glances.

This was meant for us. He is *our* Rabbit.

Finally the signal has come. The White Rabbit will lead us back home down the rabbit hole. We are sick of this world. It's harsh and grim, devoid of madness and tea parties. My hands are red and sore from the wash water and Hans is rarely lucid anymore from the poisonous fumes of hat-making. We can't hold out much longer.

When Hans inhales the felting fumes, he sees things, and sometimes he can make those things come true.

That very evening we set out for the palace. Hans takes a leather bag with a mercury-treated length of felt. I bring stale bread.

It's a long walk from our small house behind the Peat Market to the King's residence, but it's June, and we can't help but feel happy thinking of the soon-to-be-transformed King. We skip hand-in-hand through the wooded park that leads to the palace, under a full moon that makes my brother madder than ever. I pluck white and green lilies to weave him a garland. Hans finds it hard to speak these days, but his magic is strong. He swings the garland into the sky. It whirls up and up, glittering, until it settles among the stars. A heavenly crown for our Rabbit King.

I drop crumbs of my stale bread along our meandering route to mislead our enemies. When my feet start to ache in their wooden clogs, I take them off to run barefoot through the lush grass.

The royal palace dreams amidst beautiful gardens like ruched skirts, colorless under the moonlight.

We don't dare enter through the big front doors. Instead, we run giddily around the palace until we find another entrance, overlooking the pond. The sentry has nodded off; the doors are open to the mild night. And presto, we're in the King's bedroom. Clearly he doesn't fear us.

The King lies in his silk bedclothes on an enormous golden four-poster. The wooden floor is so shiny I can almost see myself in it. He snores a little. At this point, he's just a man.

Hans stuffs his face into the leather bag with its mercury-drenched felt. His eyes wheel like stars as his head comes up. "You, King," he says in his light stuttering voice, "you are the White Rabbit falling down the well, and all the King's men won't make you whole again."

The King transforms before our eyes. His big French nose becomes a white, whiskered muzzle. His fluffy paws stretch and scrabble in a rabbity dream; his pink nose twitches and snuffles.

We wait respectfully for the Rabbit to wake up. We don't want him in a bad mood. When birds start singing, we realize that the White Rabbit won't lead us anywhere this night. Clogs in one hand, skirts in the other, I tiptoe back out into the rose garden. Hans staggers after me. I'm thankful he's still clutching his bag. Mercury is expensive, and we couldn't easily replace it if we lost it.

I want to feel elated, to dance as we did on our way in, but my feet hurt, and we're both tired, let down. We hoped to be going home right away. It's been so long.

When it's fully light, we wake in our beds in this world and must go to work. Nothing's changed, except that the Butcher's gone. "He said he was just going out to buy some tobacco!" his wife wails.

Weeks later, the White Rabbit hasn't yet summoned us. When we hear the King's taking a tour around town, we leave work to watch the procession. The King, French nose and all, sits in his golden coach, waving affably to his subjects. He's no longer a rabbit.

At last it dawns on me. "Hans, he just wasn't *our* Rabbit. We made a mistake. He was someone else's Rabbit."

Hans opens his eyes wide. The vortexes swirl. If only we could enter them without a guide! "The Butcher," he says. "He was the Butcher's Rabbit."

Of course. That explains everything. The Butcher was standing next to us when the King said the magic words. This gives me so much hope. People are going home, rescue rabbits *are* being sent.

I take my brother's arm. We will get home, see the Caterpillar again, play croquet with the Queen.... We're just going to have to wait our turn.

Rabbit Study

by Bathsheba Veghte

Midnight After Winter-Long Rains

by Peter Munro

When everything is dry at last
and all the dripping stopped,
when lichen-draggled branches cast
shadows across a crop
of moss decades in the making, listen
to the Swainson's thrush piping its lesson.

Sitka spruce filter the long light.
The darkness they shelter
remains alive all through the night
sun of summer. Burnished
jewel-bright, a ruby-crowned kinglet sings
and dusk gathers ravens in its wings.

Hemlocks needle this bed of moss.
Raven pinions whisper,
ghosting past the tidings of loss
filtered through our kisses.
Trace your fingers across my skin. Erase
what winters within my most secret place.

On Leave

by Henry Hu

A Man and a River

by Megan Tilley

The witch that lived near the river was not to be messed with. Everyone in the town knew that. It was just as accepted as gravity, or church on Sundays. Kids threw rocks at the grand houses on the rich side of town or shot pellet guns at store windows, but they never went down to the river, never made their way through the dripping ferns that would've left streaks of damp on their clothes in accusations of trespass. When the paved road went through, even it curved like a fat gray serpent away from the witch's house.

The witch had always been there, that much was agreed upon. Where the witch came from or what the witch looked like couldn't be settled on. Those who had been in the town the longest said it was an old woman, long hair piled on her head and pierced through with bones and crow feathers. They said she only went out in the night, and that she stole the laundry of those destined to drown in the river's depths or be dashed to pieces on the rocks. When people in the town found laundry missing, fear would lay a cold hand on them, and they avoided the river like it would swallow them whole.

When the salesman appeared in the town, the townspeople didn't pay him any mind— they'd had plenty of his like over the years. He moved house to house on the road, selling booze and bleach, and beads the color of the sky. Yards of beautiful cotton prints spilled from the trunk of his car. Packets of seeds filled wilting cardboard boxes, nestled near the sharp heads of gardening tools.

Within weeks, the women of the town had new dresses in cobalt and ivory and lavender, strings of beads in their hair and around their wrists, handkerchiefs white as clouds. Their husbands planted new varieties of seeds and grew fat red tomatoes, and cucumbers as long as their forearms. Shining hatchets hung in garages and sheds.

"You've sold to almost everyone in town," Norton the electrician said, palming a bottle of liquor in his hand as the salesman tucked the money into his back pocket. "Ain't you gonna run out of things to sell soon?"

"Almost everyone?" the salesman asked, slamming the trunk of the car. He was low on liquor and hatchets and seeds and beads, but he had never left a town without selling at least one thing to everyone in it.

"Well, there's the witch," Norton the electrician said and smiled wide to show bare gums. When he was younger, he'd gotten wires crossed rewiring the church, and his teeth had turned black and dropped out of his gums like pearls from charred oysters.

"The witch?" the salesman asked, and pushed his hat farther up on his brow. "What witch?"

"The town witch," Norton the electrician said. "Every town has a witch."

The salesman, of course, had sold to a great number of town witches. Usually, they were just old women who chased children out of their yards with threats to rip out their eyes in their sleep, promised curses on grocery store clerks when they packed the cold items right in with dry...or they were just lonely. He could handle town witches.

Norton the electrician had given him some directions but had warned him of the muddy tracks, low branches, and thick brambles. He told him the witch had been prying up the road with crowbars she stole from the mechanics just up the road from the turn-off, but the salesman expected the boggy terrain itself was harder on the road than whatever old woman lived out near the river.

When the salesman's car got stuck in the mud, he got out, pushed his hat back, and packed ferns and twigs underneath the tires so they had something solid to back onto. When the low branches scratched the top of his car, he stretched the last of his white muslin over the top and secured it with twine to protect the paint. Where the brambles had overgrown the track and caught at his tires, he cut them back with the last of the hatchets until the blade was dull and all the brambles laid aside.

Set behind dripping birches, the house's sagging front porch was supported by ropes tied to trees. Burnt-out Christmas lights snaked around the tree trunks. Bird bones wrapped in fishing line dangled from the gutters like wind chimes. A dog sat on the porch, snoozing in the summer heat. When the salesman slammed his car door shut, the dog opened one lazy eyelid, took a long look, and dropped back to sleep.

The salesman straightened his shirt, took off his hat to smooth down his hair, and approached the house. The front steps were decorated with curious symbols in faded blue paint, the same paint that was used to cover the peeling porch ceiling. From the open window came the scratchy strains of the blues.

The salesman knocked on the door and a muffled thump came from inside. The door opened and a child stared at the salesman from just behind the doorframe. The salesman's brows rose in surprise. The child's eyes were clouded over, set deep above sallow cheeks. One hand wrapped around the doorframe, nails long and black with lacquer. A threadbare silk robe was tied around its waist, tattered lace decorating the sleeves.

"Hello," the salesman said, forcing a grin over his teeth. "I just finished my rounds in town, and someone mentioned you lived out here, and I was wondering if I could interest you in some new wares. Do you mind getting your mother for me?"

"I am the mother," the child said, its voice like water pouring over rocks, low in its throat, betraying its age.

The salesman cleared his throat. "I see. The townspeople just said that you might be interested in some—"

"The townspeople are fools," the witch said. It left the door open behind it as it moved to stand on the porch. A dirty mirror on the far wall seen through the doorway revealed a sagging couch and a sewing machine. The machine was threaded with something black—thick thread or human hair. The salesman shivered.

"I see you sew," the salesman said and gestured at the reflection.

The witch blinked.

"I have some beautiful fabric. I'm out of muslin, but you could still make a dress, or maybe a table cloth," he said, moving his head to see more of the room beyond, able to just make out a dark wood table that stood precariously on four different legs. Its surface was slick with dark liquid, which dripped onto the floor below. "All the women in town have new dresses now. Wouldn't be fair if you didn't get one too."

The witch pulled its robe tighter around itself. "I am not a woman and I have no need for new clothing," it said. "Did the townspeople not warn you about me?"

The salesman dropped the smile. "They did. They said you were a witch. But I'm not interested in what you are. I just know I have some fine things to sell, and anyone can use some fine things. I've sold to other town witches before."

The witch stepped closer and narrowed its murky eyes. The salesman backed up, almost falling down the porch stairs. "I am not a witch," it said.

The salesman cleared his throat. "But you –"

The witch spat off the porch, its spit dark. "They call me that in the town. I have been here since before anyone was called witch, and I will remain long after. I give those in the town something to fear in the dark, keep them away from my river.... But, let me see what fine things you have."

The salesman unrolled bolts of beautiful fabric and the witch rubbed them all between its fingers mutely. He showed the witch the blunt hatchet and promised to sharpen it. The witch pointed to its own hatchet, blade edge glinting in the afternoon sun. The salesman showed the witch the bleach, the sky-beads, the liquor. To each it stayed impassive while its milky eyes followed his every movement.

"Nothing catches your eye?" the salesman asked after the last of his wares had been brought out. The witch picked up a bead and held it up to the now-fading sunlight.

"Glass breaks," it said. "Fabric tears. Hatchets dull. Bleach dilutes. Liquor sours. All impermanent, all empty. You are a seller of illusion."

The salesman looked around at the witch's decayed house, at the bones and lights, at the broken lawn chair, and at the rusted pump dripping river water like an hourglass marking the minutes in steady tack tacks. "You need nothing," he said.

The witch shook its head and raised one sharp-nailed finger. "I desire nothing," it said. "I have a river. I have a dog. I have a house. I have a town that fears me and leaves me alone. What else ought I want in this cruel world of ours?"

The salesman pushed his hat higher up on his brow in defeat. "Well, I'm sorry to have taken up so much of your time," he said. "You have a pleasant evening."

The witch followed him to his car, the dog shambling at its heels. The salesman offered his hand, and the witch took it. Its palms were surprisingly cool.

"I'll come back with something you want," the salesman said. "I've never not sold to someone before, and I'm not about to lose my streak."

The witch took a step back and, silhouetted in sunset, watched as he drove away.

*

The salesman came back every year and bore magazine subscriptions, stained glass, necklaces, rings, kites, scarves, and cloth of every color. The people of the town grew used to him, and he learned all their names. "There goes the witch's salesman," the old folks would say. They sat out on their porches and watched their grandchildren chase each other down hot asphalt streets, the river glimmering in the distance. "He'll never learn, that one."

Each year the witch would wait in its yard while its dog loped towards the car, red tongue lolling. The salesman stayed a little longer each time, and the witch showed him how to spot eddies in the current, what mosses he could eat. It taught him how to clean a fish and they squatted together over the carcass, their hands and wrists slick with blood. He learned that the symbols on the steps were runes, and he understood their meaning. In turn, the salesman told the witch about the wars, about his children, the way the sun caught skyscrapers tall as giants. He showed the witch books about atoms and cells, and the witch spat and told him it'd like to keep the mysteries it had left.

"You're a real witch aren't you? I mean really," the salesman said many years into their friendship. The witch eyed him and returned to tending the fire. A chicken twisted on a spit and its skin cracked and oozed clear juices.

"I am not a witch, child. You should know that by now," it said. "I come from the river, and the river comes from me. We are one and the same. They've called me all manner of names, witch among them. But I am me, and it is me, and we are one, and you'll keep a civil tongue in your mouth if you expect me to buy anything."

But the witch never bought anything from him. No beads or buttons, strings or skillets, liquor or lotion. The salesman grew old but never stopped coming. And the witch still waited for him. It made him a chair out of bowed branches so that he had something comfortable to sit on, and it brewed him tea out of roots and leaves that tasted bitter, but helped his memory.

The witch grew older too. Its resplendent smooth skin turned a delicate crepe, its graceful fingers curled like fiddleheads. While the rest of it aged, its eyes brightened, until irises of startling green, like moss-covered rock, emerged.

When the salesman missed a year, and then another, the witch carried on with its old ways, cooking its fish and casting its spells for rain and flood and thunder, though more often than not, the weather did what it wanted.

One day, a car pulled up in front of the house. The witch had grown used to the quiet—the rumble of the motor made its skin prickle in irritation. The witch stepped onto the creaking porch. The salesman's car sat in the yard. But when the door opened, not a salesman, but a boy got out. He was carrying a box. The witch's dog bared its teeth at the stranger.

"Are you the witch?" the boy asked.

The witch gave a sharp jerk of its head, opened its mouth to argue over the name he had given it.

"My father said I could find you here."

"You're the salesman's boy," the witch said. Its voice creaked from disuse.

The boy nodded.

"Your father never sold me a thing, and you aren't likely to either."

"I'm not here to sell you anything," the boy said. "Besides, I'm not as good a salesman as he was. He could sell a lie to a liar. He left some things for you, though, in his will."

"I don't want it," the witch said, and turned away.

"You can throw it out then," the boy said. "But you should take it anyway."

The boy set the box on the ground. "I'm just going to leave it here," he said, then drove away.

The box sat in the witch's yard overnight. The dog nosed at it, and let out a small whine, but came when the witch called it away.

In the morning, the witch opened the box. Inside was a sketch of the witch, hunched over a fire. A handful of blue beads rattled around the bottom of the box, a dirt-streaked scrap of muslin was twined around a dull hatchet.

The witch cried for the first time in as far as it could remember. Its tears left rivulets that ran through the dirt to the river. The witch carried the box down to the rocky bank, and let the hatchet, the beads, and the muslin slide into the water. It tucked the picture into its robe over its heart, and there it remained, until the roads came too close. When the bulldozer knocked down the last stand of trees, the witch slipped into the river too, dissolving into streaks of foam. The picture stayed on the mossy rocks, caught on some bare roots, until the rains came and washed it into the river, where it too disappeared in time.

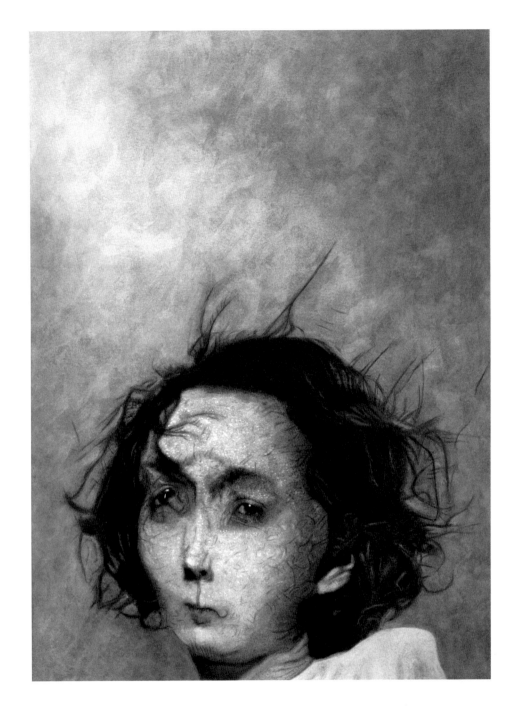

Juliet
by Caren McCaleb

The Fifth Season

by Emily Stoddard

Bees have claimed the pear tree,
and now

the backyard hums
as we examine what remains,

consider recovery.
My grandmother is at my heels, meshing

her feet into rotten pears, tempting
the bees with the soft edges

of exposed ankles.
Her mind more shadow

than flower blossom, she is becoming
the muddy door between winter and spring.

My father shakes his head,
rounds the tree again.

I await diagnosis,
begin to mourn

the hole that will form
if the tree comes down, but

my grandmother leans into me,
whispers—*It's not dead. Not yet.*

Is it possible then—

that everything decays,
but not everything rots?

Later that day, I find her
in the garage

playing a piano that waits

to go into storage.

She has never learned how to play,
but here is the piano, singing

a song of her own design,
and now

she is humming.

The Green Pear

by Anita K. Boyle

On the sunlit sill, a green pear
begins to blush. It's been ripening
for days. Forever. The pear
was picked too soon, for fear
it would turn to mush. But in fact,
the meat is hard as stone.

Wrapped in paper and tucked
into darkness, the cruelty
of a sour pear sweetens in time.
But this is a waste of beauty.

The pear tree grows in the foothills
where cool rains wash
the orchard clean. The grove
is like a close-knit family,
and follows the valley, as does a river.

There, the air opens to the sound of flickers
calling, a fitful knock on wood.
Sunlight sugars the pear, a ladle of luster.

Essential Needlework Advice for Shadows, Spectres, and other Ethereal Beings

by Rachel Linn

To make yourself a body from scratch, first you need to find a needle. Sharp or dull, with a head or an eye or without. Of a suitable length. Hooked? Possibly. You won't need a thimble until you have fingers, and, if this is your first attempt, you may not make it to the tips before unraveling. Don't get ahead of yourself.

It is best to start from your insides and work outward, for example, by weaving a sturdy armature that can be wrinkled or stepped on for years without becoming inflexible or threadbare. A rug, hooked or braided, might work. Remnants of fabric and yarn will also do, or a wool sweater felted, accidentally or on purpose, in the dryer. Lung of cardigan, heart of mitten, nerves of lace! No one will be able to see inside you, if all goes well, so it is unnecessary to use complimentary colors or prints. Your mismatching collection of shank buttons and toggles that were once sewn into clothing tags (meant to replace any ones lost from the primary set on a garment), can represent valves or alveoli.

Then, knit yourself a covering; cables, knots, fringe. Choose a thick yarn for this part, worsted weight or larger, to avoid thinness of skin, and knit using small needles to create a tight stitch that will allow nothing to come through. Leave an opening for a zipper along one side, concealed under an arm. Left or right, your preference.

Now come the most daunting decisions. Do you want your corporeal self to have eyes, ears, nails, a mouth? To be merely a vague, nebulous presence, or to have the sharp lines and details of an individual?

Remember, once you've made yourself a body, it may have a mind of its own. Its linty consciousness could discover how to make and use tools, and then redesign its skin in clashing stripes of color or tattoos of cross stitch. It might learn to quilt, expanding itself in every direction with layers of batting and appliqué. It might decide to wash on hot and then refuse to reshape and lie flat to dry, pinning itself to a clothesline in bright sunlight to whip and snap in the wind.

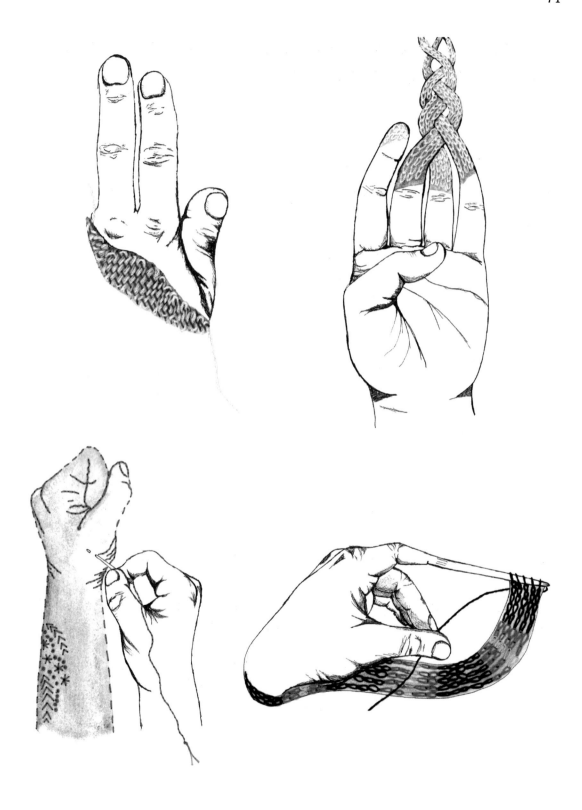

Runaway

by Claire Hermann

I travel in the burned-out shells of old sedans,
braid larkspur and oak leaves in my tangled hair.
I rest in broken chairs fallen from trucks beside the highways,
shelter from rain beneath the rusted roofs of old tobacco barns.
I eat only the color of clear sky and clouds at sunset,
drink only the smell of honeysuckle in roadside hedges.
Don't be surprised if you wake up and find me licking your roses,
or wrapping the sheet of your house's shadow around my shoulders.
I won't be stopping long. I'll keep moving.
At night I sleep beneath a blanket, not of stars,
but of the darkness between them.

Knit one Pearl one

by Ellie Davies

Through Earth and Sky

by Gwendolyn Kiste

If they listened, they'd know your people don't live in pointed tents. Some don't live at all, invisible like ghosts, reduced to kitschy feather knickknacks kept on mantles.

If they listened, they'd know you and your sister have no mantle or anything else besides a loan on a mattress more rust than springs, faded linens the color of urine. You don't even own the clothes on your back. The women do, the ones with tight-knit mouths and rulers always ready to smack wayward fingers. They own you too and own the other children who saw their parents vanish, dead before their time. The way it goes with people like you.

If they listened, they'd know you like magic, the same magic all kids share—secrets you keep, wishes you make, silly incantations you recite to the darkness where no one can hear.

But here inside these walls where lonely children live, you aren't supposed to care about spells or magnetic sand or dream catchers in windows. Magic can't be yours. That's what the unsmiling women tell you.

"Besides," they say, "it's a cliché that your people like magic. You don't want to be a cliché, do you?"

Yet magic is all you have.

If they listened, they'd know what happens when children have nothing else. What they do have becomes more powerful, more potent than it would be in a happy child's hands, a child with two parents and a pretty house and a baby doll that cries 'Mama.' You and your sister have no baby dolls, but you have each other, and together, your words, your wishes, your secrets become real. A sunny day when you say so. A ruler broken in two before it reaches your cheeks. Little things, insignificant things, the only things that matter.

Soon you grow older and can't recall what your childhood secrets were, but the wind remembers for you. The wind is your companion, and it never turns you away. It always listens.

And the wind is a good listener.

If they listened, they'd know why two girls with no family except each other marry the first men who will have them. The cruel women give you no other choice, but matrimony brings a different kind of rules and rulers. In this mining town, faces and hands and men become hard and weathered, and the black ash of West Virginia blankets everything, inside and out.

On your wedding day, you can hardly see the men's faces—they're caked too thick with dirt and dust. Not even your magic can fix that.

If they listened, they'd know love cannot be captured in a potion, no matter how hard you try, and when your hair is a gloss of black and skin a perfect copper, love will only come after years of marriage, if it comes at all.

Even once they claim they love you, the men won't let you forget how you're lucky to have them, lucky to bask in the glow of their pale skin, however sullied from years of work. Being near them will make you whiter, won't it?

If they listened, they wouldn't wave you off when you rail against your sister's husband.

"He goes to work, day after day," they say, "and that's enough."

But the glint in his eye—that wandering eye—says it's not enough, not when he quaffs a bottle of cheap whiskey instead of bringing home his pay, not when that whiskey boils inside him, coursing through his veins like fire, not when he raises his hand to your only sister and brings it down again and again until her skin is a constellation of welts.

Together, your magic could overwhelm him, but she won't make a wish against her husband.

"I'm his wife," she says. "I can't betray him."

If they listened, they'd try to help you. But they don't listen. Only the man you loathe notices you, how the wind wraps around you as you fill your sister's pockets with smoky quartz, desperate to protect her.

"Witch," her husband says, and you smile.

If they listened, they'd know magic is imperfect. Sometimes, it fails, especially when a spell needs two. And you no longer have two. Your sister disappears into the night without a word. There is no body. He hides it well.

The hills of West Virginia hide it for him.

"He did this to her," you tell them, but they don't listen. She's just another tally mark, vanished with the rest, dead before her time. The way it goes with people like you.

If they listened, those with the fine carriages and finer lace, they'd know justice is more than a gavel and a courtroom and a man yelling 'Order!' Here in your house no more than a shack, justice is a pot on a stove and the remnants of a chicken. You ate the meat last week, but that doesn't mean the leftovers—the blood and the bones— can't still do some good.

If they listened, they'd know the recipe you use to raise your sister's bones, bring her through earth and sky, bring her home to you. While your husband and children dream their lazy dreams, her bones sit with you at the rickety hand-me-down table. Her bones tell you secrets. These are secrets you and she will never forget.

Her husband runs because he knows those secrets are no longer safe. After all, a witch can't be trusted.

If they listened, they'd know magic pays distance no mind. It doesn't take long for the wind to find him, and a little bit at a time, his ulcerated guts tie into knots. He must suffer as you suffer, slowly and without end. At night, you can hear him scream, over blue-green mountains and valleys built from coal and sweat.

If they listened, they could hear him too. But they don't listen, and this time, it's probably good. Because if they heard him scream and knew you were to blame, they'd burn you on the nearest pyre.

If they listened, they'd know you leave that mining town. Your husband earns a good job by the sea, and while you'll miss those hills that brought your sister back to you, albeit for one night, you won't miss the stink of death and the cinders that permeate everyone and everything there. Before you leave, you drive past the building, the prison, where you and your sister stayed as kids. It's converted to offices now.

If they listened, they'd know your children grow and have children of their own, but your mind never strays far from the place you left behind. Where others smell the salt of the ocean, you can remember only the acrid stench of smog. Your sister should be here with you instead of in the earth where you laid her bones. She rests but you cannot. The wounds inside you never close.

Faraway, her husband's guts remain in knots, but his life continues, and he eyes another young wife whose face his fists will mar. He never changes, so you must be the one to change him. It is your duty to protect those like your sister, those who can't protect themselves. You muster every bit of magic left in you and ask the wind to cross a thousand miles. A stalwart friend, it obliges. Her husband screams out a final time and then retreats to silence even blacker than coal. The past is bones now and nothing more. In your fine house, no longer a shack, you recline in your rocking chair, smiling to yourself. At last, you feel complete—or as complete as you'll ever be without your sister. Your partner in magic lost forever.

But a new partner is waiting, his chestnut eyes staring up at you.

If they listened, they'd know about your grandson. Whenever he misbehaves, you laugh and put the evil eye on him, your gaze narrowed, your gnarled hands suspended in the air, but you don't scare him. He just giggles and scurries away. It never occurs to him how strange it is his grandmother's a witch. He accepts it like the wind and the sun and the color of your hair—bolts of nighttime hidden inside the gray. His grandmother is gray and she is a witch. These things are the same in his eyes, and neither one is wrong.

If they listened, they'd know that little boy with the ornery grin gives you hope. You watch him speak to trees.

You watch the wind protect him. You protect him too, but you won't always be here. The earth and the sky will, and they'll care for him well.

If they listened, they'd know all these things and more, a world beyond, so much greater than them and greater than you. But they don't listen. And they never will.

Your secrets remain with the wind.

"the faithful flock 2"

by Michael Marsh

A Few Words Left Behind

by Jeff Hardin

I've no desire to use a different voice with you
than with a white oak sapling, moss I walk upon,
or creek stones. Even a falling leaf describes a prayer.

When bewilderment descends, I give up searching for
my hidden name, the one the willow snaps along its lengths.
I turn back toward the fencerow, its six or seven posts.

Imagine a language pieced together from archaic words
we thought we left behind. I could spend all evening
staring at two trees at the far end of this snow-soaked field.

Our people years ago would plant an apple tree
some distance from the house to draw the bugs away.
A lesson's there for those who keep life's sweetness near.

The cold's moved in to cancel what we've stored away.
Will we make the spring? It's envy I have—but also
love—for how the grasshopper gets to fling itself away.

Sycamore

by David Constantine

You feel the whole thing in the bid for it

The days of seed-cast must have been quite still
There's so much here not much can have gone down the wind

A tree coming into her own through years of room
Putting up, putting out, like a river
Ascending out of the waters under the earth
Feeling into finer and finer tributaries
Fingering the air
Already in April working up her progeny

And below, under the skirts, in the dappled shape of her
All the life above is being emulated
Testa, radicle, plumule
Till all the zone below is softly jostling
And the one is manifold
Each frail more-light-desiring cotyledon gapes
And through, across, comes a likeness in strengthening bronze
The idea of a tree is building
All the ground is prickling
Dense as a swarm, shoal, murmuration
As though every one in the gush of seed had taken
Every winged seed-head went home
And knows it wants to breathe

You see none of this on the urban concrete
And precious little in the parks and gardens
And this itself is only a visitant
Like a snowfall
It will disembody
It was an interlude, we were passing, we happened to witness it
Milt
Stardust

Fierce maledicted Lilith howling down the four winds
I have a forest in every seed of me...

Between the Trees

by Ellie Davies

Enough

by T. Clear

Winter, and I step outside
in the last minutes before dusk.

All day I've huddled
head-down beneath a lamp

and fog has hoarded the sun
until now, when light

angles across the garden
and ignites the red-furred limbs

of the sumac so briefly
I know I have everything

I will ever need.

Contributors

Olivia V. Ambrogio

Olivia V. Ambrogio's work has been published in over twenty-five journals and anthologies, including *Sugar Mule, Electric Velocipede, Café Irreal*, and *Fugue*. A native Detroiter, she headed east to get a Ph.D. studying the sex lives of marine snails. In spite of the surprising allure of this research field, she ended up in science communication in the D.C. area and does writing and photography whenever she can.

Bo Balder

Bo Balder is the first Dutch author to have been published in *Clarkesworld* and *The Magazine of Fantasy and Science Fiction*. Her short fiction has also appeared in *Escape Pod, Nature,* and other places. Her sci-fi novel *The Wan* was published by Pink Narcissus Press. Visit her website: boukjebalder.nl

Anita K. Boyle

Anita K. Boyle is an artist and poet whose works are inspired by the natural and manmade landscape of the Pacific Northwest. Her poems can be found in books—*What the Alder Told Me, The Drenched, Bamboo Equals Loon*; anthologies such as *WA 129* (Sage Hill Press 2017), *Last Call* and *Ice Cream Poems* (World Enough Writers 2018, 2017); and literary magazines including *Clover, The Raven Chronicles*, and *Crab Creek Review*. She publishes handmade limited-edition books featuring poets of Washington State at Egress Studio just outside Bellingham, WA.

KT Bryski

KT Bryski is a Canadian author, podcaster, and playwright. Her short fiction has appeared in *Strange Horizons, Apex*, and *Daily Science Fiction* (among others), and her audio dramas are available wherever fine podcasts are found. She is a Parsec winner, Sunburst finalist, and Stonecoast MFA alum. KT lives in Toronto with a strongly opinionated cat. Visit her at ktbryski.com.

Constantinos Chaidalis

Constantinos Chaidalis is a multidisciplinary designer from Athens, Greece. He works as a creative director and motion graphics designer for advertising agencies and production houses. He usually works for TV commercials, sometimes working on compositing, direction, matte painting and design. He also works as a director for theatrical video installations and as a graphic designer/illustrator. His self-initiated projects are usually experimental and very personal—mostly collage and mixed media compositions and their animated versions. Technically he tries to experiment as much as he can with new digital media and software and also with traditional creative media (screen printing, traditional animation, video, photography). Constantinos lives with his cat, Bikini.

T. Clear

A co-founder of Floating Bridge Press, T. Clear's poetry has appeared in many magazines and anthologies, most recently in *Terrain.org*, *Scoundrel Time*, *UCity Review*, *Rise Up Review*, and *56 Days of August/Poetry Postcards*. Her work has been nominated for a Pushcart Prize and an Independent Best American Poetry Award. She is a lifelong resident of Seattle, facilitates the Easy Speak critique group Re/Write, and has the good fortune to spend her days inventing new color combinations to paint on sandblasted glass.

David Constantine

David Constantine, born 1944 in Salford, Lancashire, was a university teacher of German language and literature for thirty years. He has published a dozen volumes of poetry, including *Elder* (2014); two novels, *Davies* (1985) and *The Life-Writer* (2015); and five collections of short stories. He is an editor and translator of Hölderlin, Goethe, Kleist, and Brecht. His new and greatly expanded edition of *Friedrich Hölderlin Selected Poetry*, was published by Bloodaxe in 2018, around the same time as *The Collected Poems of Bertolt Brecht*, translated with Tom Kuhn, from Norton USA. For his stories he won the BBC National and the Frank O' Connor International Awards (2010, 2013). The film *45 Years* was based on his story "In Another Country." He edited *Modern Poetry in Translation* from 2003 to 2014 with Helen Constantine.

Ellie Davies

Ellie Davies (Born 1976) lives in Dorset and works in the woods and forests of Southern England. She gained her MA in Photography from London College of Communication in 2008. Davies is represented by Patricia Armocida Gallery in Milan, Susan Spiritus Gallery in Newport Beach, A.Galerie in Paris and Brussels, Sophie Maree Gallery in The Netherlands, Brucie Collections in Kiev, and Crane Kalman Brighton Gallery in the UK. Davies launched her newest series, *Fires, 2018*, at Photo London 2018 with Crane Kalman Brighton Gallery at Somerset House in May. *Fires 2* was recently selected Winner of the Urbanautica Institute Awards 2018: Nature, Environment and Perspectives. Other recent solo exhibitions include *Her Feet Planted Firmly on the Ground* at The Houston Center of Photography from March 2017, and a solo exhibition entitled *Into the Woods* at the Roe Valley Arts and Cultural Centre in Northern Ireland in April 2017.

Bryce Emley

Bryce Emley is the author of the prose chapbook *Smoke and Glass* (Folded Word, 2018), and his poetry and prose can be found in *The Atlantic, Narrative, Boston Review, Prairie Schooner, Best American Experimental Writing*, etc. He works in marketing at the University of New Mexico Press and is Poetry Editor of *Raleigh Review*. Read more at bryceemley.com.

Vanessa Fogg

Vanessa Fogg dreams of selkies, dragons, and gritty cyberpunk futures from her home in western Michigan. She spent years as a research scientist in molecular cell biology and now works as a freelance medical writer. Her fiction has appeared in *Liminal Stories, Daily Science Fiction, GigaNotoSaurus*, and more. She is fueled by green tea. For a complete bibliography and more, visit her website at vanessafogg.com. She is erratically active on Twitter at @FoggWriter.

Cicely Gill

Cicely Gill lives on a very green Scottish island and tries to make writing the first thing she does each day. She has self-published a book of her poetry, *The Trees of Childhood*, and two detective novels, *Ivory* and *Zara on Arran*. Her plays have been performed on Arran and in Glasgow. When not writing, she spends her time trying to keep the brambles and bracken from entering the house.

Sierra Golden

Sierra Golden graduated with an MFA in poetry from North Carolina State University. Her manuscript *The Slow Art* won the Dorothy Brunsman Poetry Prize and was published by Bear Star Press in 2018. Golden's poems appear in literary journals such as *Prairie Schooner*, *Permafrost*, and *Ploughshares*. She has been awarded fellowships and residencies by Hedgebrook, Hugo House, and The Elizabeth George Foundation. Although she calls Washington State home, Golden spent many summers in Alaska, working as a commercial fisherman. She now works in communications at Casa Latina, a nonprofit organization in Seattle that advances the power and well-being of Latino immigrants.

Amanda Greive

Amanda Greive graduated with a bachelor's degree in visual arts from the University of Illinois at Springfield and has exhibited her work at RJD Gallery in Bridgehampton, New York, Arcadia Contemporary in Los Angeles, Abend Gallery in Denver, Woman Made Gallery in Chicago, and the Rockford Art Museum in Rockford, Illinois. Most recently, she was a finalist in the 2017 *Figurativas* exhibit in Barcelona and was also a finalist in the 12th International ARC Salon, having been awarded an Arcadia Contemporary award. She is currently represented by RJD Gallery.

Jeff Hardin

Jeff Hardin is the author of five collections of poetry, most recently *Small Revolution* and *No Other Kind of World* (recipient of the X. J. Kennedy Prize). His work has also been honored with the Nicholas Roerich Prize and the Donald Justice Poetry Prize. His sixth collection, *A Clearing Space in the Middle of Being*, will appear in fall 2019. Recent poems appear in *The Hudson Review, North American Review, Southern Review, Chattahoochee Review, The Cortland Review*, and others.

Lucy Harlow

Lucy Harlow grew up in England and Hong Kong and currently lives in Philadelphia. Her fiction and poetry have appeared or are forthcoming in *Aliterate, Isacoustic, Strange Horizons*, and others. She is a PhD student at Princeton University and is working on a dissertation about riddles and ruins in medieval and early modern literature.

Jana Heidersdorf

Jana Heidersdorf is an illustrator of the feral and fantastical located in Berlin. In surreal, moody mixed media compositions, her work explores everything lurking in the dark and unseen, may it be creatures, feelings or fairytales. When she's not drawing you can find her dabbling in the dark arts of writing and photography or stalking the local bird population.

Claire Hermann

Claire Hermann has had work selected as finalist for the North Carolina Poet Laureate's Award and as *Split This Rock* Poem of the Week. Her poems have appeared in such publications as *Borderlands: Texas Poetry Journal, Lines + Stars, Southern Women's Poetry Review*, and *Prime Number Magazine*. She has a weakness for cats, farmers markets, foggy mornings, and justice.

Henry Hu

Hong Kong bred, Sydney based, Henry Hu's artworks are personal and mercurial, with a focus on storytelling. He assembles a series of works piece by piece. By experimenting with digital tools, he commits to linkages between the peculiar and the familiar. Style can vary within a series, a recurring structure holding the series coherent. henryhhu.com

Kathryn Hunt

Kathryn Hunt makes her home on the coast of the Salish Sea. Her poems have appeared in *Coal Hill Review*, *The Sun*, *Rattle*, *Radar*, *Orion*, *The Writer's Almanac*, *The Missouri Review*, and *Narrative*. Her collection of poems, *Long Way Through Ruin*, was published by Blue Begonia Press, and she's recently completed a second collection of poems, *You Won't Find It on a Map*, a finalist for the 2017 Idaho Prize from Lost Horse Press. She is the recipient of residencies and awards from PLAYA, Artists Trust, and Ucross. She made films for many years; her film *No Place Like Home* premiered at the Venice Film Festival, in Italy. She's worked as a waitress, shipscaler, short-order cook, bookseller, printer, food bank coordinator, filmmaker, and freelance writer. kathrynhunt.net

Gwendolyn Kiste

Gwendolyn Kiste is the author of the Bram Stoker Award-nominated collection *And Her Smile Will Untether the Universe*, the dark fantasy novella *Pretty Marys All in a Row*, and her debut horror novel, *The Rust Maidens*. In addition to *Bracken*, her short fiction has appeared in *Nightmare Magazine*, *Shimmer*, *Black Static*, *Daily Science Fiction*, *Interzone*, and *LampLight*, among other publications. A native of Ohio, she resides on an abandoned horse farm outside of Pittsburgh with her husband, two cats, and not nearly enough ghosts. You can find her online at gwendolynkiste.com.

Jenifer Browne Lawrence

Jenifer Browne Lawrence is the author of *Grayling* and *One Hundred Steps from Shore*. Awards include the Perugia Press Prize, the Orlando Poetry Prize, the James Hearst Poetry Prize, the *Potomac Review* Poetry Award, and a Washington State Artist Trust GAP grant. Her work appears in *The Los Angeles Review, Narrative, North American Review, Rattle,* and elsewhere. Jenifer lives on the west side of Puget Sound and edits *Crab Creek Review*.

Rachel Linn

Rachel Linn holds an MFA in creative writing from the University of Washington, where she received the Eugene Van Buren Prize for her thesis project. Her writing and illustrations have appeared or are forthcoming in the St. Louis Arts in Transit Metrolines & Metroscapes programs, *Rivet, Small Po[r]tions, Typehouse, Storm Cellar,* and elsewhere. She is currently helping to plan the 2019 St. Louis Small Press Expo and hopes you will be there.

Michael Marsh

Michael Marsh is an amateur photographer living in the beautiful seaside town of Whitstable on the Kent coast of England. He specializes in an atmospheric, cinematic style of photography that channels his creative self through imagery born of a desire to lead the viewer on a short journey of escape from present day realities.

Caren McCaleb

Caren McCaleb is an Emmy-winning documentary editor by day and an artist by night. Her black-and-white paintings come from a multi-step process that relies on chance and intuition at each stage. She is inspired by a vivid sense of the ethereal, the realm just beyond ordinary senses. Her technical process involves both photography and painting, which is fitting as the subject veers between the real and the imaginary.

Erika Michael

Erika Michael is an art historian, painter, and poet from Woodway, Washington. Born in Vienna, raised in New York, she's lived around Seattle since 1966. As a Pratt Institute graduate, Erika worked in animation and as an abstract painter. With a University of Washington Ph.D. in art history, she taught and published in Renaissance Studies and worked in various Northwest museums. A poet for many years, Erika participated in workshops with Carolyn Forché, Linda Gregerson, Thomas Lux, Laure-Anne Bosselaar, and Tim Seibles. Her poems have appeared in *Poetica Magazine, Drash: Northwest Mosaic, Cascade: Journal of the Washington Poets Association, The Winter Anthology,* and *Belletrist Magazine*, among others.

Peter Munro

Peter Munro is a fisheries scientist who works in the Bering Sea, the Gulf of Alaska, the Aleutian Islands, and Seattle. Munro's poems have been published or are forthcoming in *Poetry, Beloit Poetry Journal, The Iowa Review, Birmingham Poetry Review, Passages North, The Cortland Review, Valparaiso Poetry Review, Compose, Rattle, The Literary Review, Carolina Quarterly*, and elsewhere. Listen to more poems at munropoetry.com.

Rebecca Hart Olander

Rebecca Hart Olander's poetry has appeared recently in *Ilanot Review, Plath Poetry Project*, and *Solstice,* and collaborative work made with Elizabeth Paul has been published in *They Said: A Multi-Genre Anthology of Contemporary Collaborative Writing* (Black Lawrence Press) and online at *Duende* and other journals. Rebecca won the 2013 Women's National Book Association Writing Contest in the Poetry Category. Her first chapbook is forthcoming from dancing girl press in fall 2019. She teaches writing at Westfield State University and is the Editor/Director of Perugia Press. Find her @ rholanderpoet and rebeccahartolander.com.

Emily Stoddard

Emily Stoddard's writing has appeared or is forthcoming in *Radar, Tinderbox Poetry Journal, New Poetry from the Midwest, Cold Mountain Review, Menacing Hedge, Gravel,* and elsewhere. She is an affiliate of the Amherst Writers & Artists Method and leads writing workshops online and in her studio based in Michigan. Learn more at emilystoddard.com.

Stephen Thom

Stephen Thom is a musician and support worker from Carrbridge in the Highlands of Scotland. His pieces have appeared in *Firewords Quarterly, Holdfast Magazine,* and *Aphotic Realm,* among others.

Megan Tilley

Born and raised in the swamps of Florida, Megan Tilley is an avid collector of teapots, bones, ferns, and ghost stories. She is a doctoral student of Audiology at the University of South Florida. Her works has appeared in *Fictionvale, The Deep Dark Woods Anthology, Undead: A Poetry Anthology of Ghosts and Ghouls*, and others.

Bathsheba Veghte

Bathsheba Veghte received her B.A. in Fine Arts from Bowdoin College, Brunswick, Maine. She worked predominantly as a printmaker in the 1990s as a guest printmaker at Trillium Graphics, Brisbane, California, and as an Artist in Residence at the Kala Institute, Berkeley, during which time she was represented by the Edith Caldwell Gallery, San Francisco. Her work is in the Permanent Collection of the San Francisco Museum of Art as well as in many collections on both coasts. She is currently exploring paintings on aluminum, a surface she finds exciting both for its rendering of luminosity and smoothness. See more of her art at bathshebaveghte.com.